Puffin

VERA PRATT AND THE BISHOP'S FALSE TEETH

The Bishop has a new chauffeur. The surprise is that she is Mrs Vera Pratt, ace-adventurer and Wally's fanatic mechanic mum! His Lordship kisses goodbye to his stately Jaguar and from now on it's fresh air and big thrills in the side-car of Vera's motorbike.

When he is asked to present the prizes at the local point-to-point he decides that a small bet on the favourite horse, Dirty Beast, might add some badly needed cash to the Palace housekeeping.

But his one moment of weakness leaves him speechless – when he is spotted by the evil Dud Cheque. Suddenly there's blackmail in the air, Vera's old enemy Captain Smoothy-Smythe is up to no good and horses and jockeys are disappearing . . .

In true style our heroine leaps into action (or on to the back of her motorbike!) and even Wally (ever the reluctant hero) gets on his bike to help save the Bishop. Action-packed adventure guaranteed!

This is the second adventure about Vera Pratt and her son Wally. The first book, also published by Puffin, is *Vera Pratt and the False Moustaches*, and is followed by *Vera Pratt and the Bald Head*.

Brough Girling was born in 1946. His previous jobs include teacher, ice-cream salesman, business man, freelance copywriter and promotions consultant. As well as writing children's books he has been Campaign Director of Readathon, the sponsored reading event that raises money for the Malcolm Sargent Cancer Fund for children, and the Head of the Children's Book Foundation at Book Trust in London, and is now the editor of the *Young Telegraph*.

Vera Pratt
and the
Bishop's False Teeth

BROUGH GIRLING

Illustrated by Tony Blundell

PUFFIN BOOKS

PUFFIN BOOKS

Published by the Penguin Group
Penguin Books Ltd, 27 Wrights Lane, London W8 5TZ, England
Penguin Books USA Inc., 375 Hudson Street, New York, New York 10014, USA
Penguin Books Australia Ltd, Ringwood, Victoria, Australia
Penguin Books Canada Ltd, 10 Alcorn Avenue, Toronto, Ontario, Canada M4V 3B2
Penguin Books (NZ) Ltd, 182–190 Wairau Road, Auckland 10, New Zealand

Penguin Books Ltd, Registered Offices: Harmondsworth, Middlesex, England

First published 1987
7 9 10 8 6

Printed in England by Clays Ltd, St Ives plc
Phototypeset in Linotron Bembo

Contents

A Bad Start for the Bishop

'I KNOW EXACTLY WHAT YOU ARE DOING,' shouted the Bishop. 'YOU'RE PINCHING MY PETROL!'

'No, I ain't!' said his new chauffeur. 'We was just checking to see that the car was OK!'

'That is a lie!' said the Bishop: and he was right.

He had just got up, and had been having a nice little walk in the grounds of his Palace before breakfast, when he had come round the corner of his garage and seen something that, if he had had any hair, would have made it stand on end. As it was, his mouth had fallen open in horror.

His car was half-way out of the garage, and behind it was a very large and dilapidated van with the words

ABC GARAGE – *for petrol and repairs*

on the side of it.

The Bishop's new chauffeur and a very grubby garage man were stooping down behind the car. They were poking a long rubber tube into the petrol tank. Near the other end of the tube was a large petrol can, and several other cans were standing round about them.

'I know exactly what you're doing!' repeated the Bishop. 'You are stealing my petrol!'

The driver, whose name was Dud Cheque, realized that he had been caught red-handed. Again.

I don't know if you have come across Dud Cheque before. If you have, you will know that he is not an attractive sight. He was called Dudley by his mother because he reminded her of the armadillos in Dudley Zoo, near Birmingham. He had the same dark, mean eyes, rounded shoulders and shuffling way of walking.

The only good thing you can say about Dud Cheque is that he is not a deceiver. He looks untrustworthy and dishonest, and that's what he is.

'I was only checking it over, to see if the petrol was good enough for Your Lordship's car, guv.'

'Don't lie to me!' said the Bishop. 'What do you take me for? A nincompoop?'

'Yes,' said Dud Cheque.

'Then you can leave my employment immediately!' shouted the Bishop, turning purple. 'You are dismissed! I only took you on because I felt sorry for you, but I don't feel sorry for you any more!'

Dud Cheque realized that he'd got the sack again. This was a pity, especially as he'd only started working for the Bishop the day before.

'And you,' said the Bishop addressing the garage man, 'can get back into that disgusting van and get off these premises this instant! I've a good mind to report you to your employer, Captain Smoothy-Smythe: he's a friend of mine, you know. I know him well!'

The Bishop can't have known Captain Smoothy-Smythe all that well, or he would have guessed that it was the Captain's idea to pinch the petrol!

The Bishop strode purposefully back indoors. By nature he was a mild, pleasant man with a round, pink face, and a round, pink body to go with it. But he knew he'd done the right thing. You can't discover your driver siphoning petrol out of your car and let him go unpunished – especially if he takes you for a nincompoop.

He went into the dining-room and lowered his large backside into a chair opposite his Lady Wife. His Lady Wife had already started her breakfast, and was tall, and thin, and haughty.

'You are looking very flustered this morning, Lord Bishop!' she remarked.

'I expect I am. I've just caught that ghastly new

chauffeur pinching petrol out of the car! So I've told him to leave. Now I'll have to advertise for another one.'

'Couldn't you do without a driver? They seem an unnecessary extravagance to me,' she commented coldly.

The Bishop pretended that he had not heard this remark, and got on with his toast. 'It's one thing after another in this job!' he thought to himself as he chewed it. 'A bishop's work is never done!'

When breakfast was over he went into his study. He began to open the morning's letters. The first one was from Colonel Thundering-Blunderer and it asked him to give away the prizes at the forthcoming point-to-point.

'Heavens above!' said the Bishop out loud. 'What do I know about point-to-points! I've never been to a horse race in my life, and they will expect me to hob-nob about betting and things like that. Oh well, I suppose it's all in a day's work!'

He took out a piece of posh writing-paper and wrote to the Colonel:

Dear Colonel Thundering-Blunderer,

Thank you for your kind letter, received today. I have much pleasure in accepting your invitation to give out the prizes at the forthcoming point-to-point.

I look forward to paying you a visit in a day or so to discuss further details of the event.

> *Yours most sincerely*
> *Your Lord Bishop*

Then the Bishop wrote a second letter, this time to the local paper, asking them to print the following advertisement:

WANTED

A THOROUGHLY RELIABLE,
TRUSTWORTHY CHAUFFEUR FOR
LOCAL BISHOP

QUITE GOOD PAY

WOULD SUIT SOMEONE WITH
MECHANICAL SKILLS

2

Mrs Pratt and Her Wally

Mrs Vera Pratt was sitting in her sitting-room, bolting a new side-car on to her motorbike.

'Wally, don't just sit there like a wally. Pass me that adjustable spanner.'

'Yes, Mum,' said Wally Pratt.

'I don't know: you kids today just seem to hang around doing nothing! Here's me with little or no money left, a house to run, the garden to keep tidy, and a Yamaha XG-550 to keep clean and road-worthy! I was up all hours last night cleaning out the gasket covers and welding the tappets. I spend my life cleaning and mending, and all you do is watch telly!'

Mrs Pratt's comments were justified. Wally is a large youth who never does more than he needs to. Although he has been known to do heroic things, he is not an active type of hero. He is nothing like Superman.

'Sorry, Mum, it's just that I'm not really into motorbikes – perhaps I'm not old enough.'

'Don't be daft, Wally. When I was your age I'd stripped down my first Norton 250, and could change a pair of front forks with one hand tied behind my back! Kids these days . . .' she muttered, wiping her greasy brow with an oily tea towel.

'Couldn't we get a car, Mum, like other people? You enjoyed it when we had that Jaguar,' suggested Wally, rather timidly.

'No, Wallace!' she said emphatically. 'My motorcar days are over. I have gone back to good old motorbikes. They are cheaper to run than cars and much more practical. How could I bring a car into the kitchen to re-condition its gearbox? With a motorbike it's easy!'

'But bikes are so uncomfortable, Mum.'

'Now look here, Wally!' said his mother, putting her hands on her black-leather hips in a determined way. 'Once I've got this two-seater side-car bolted on, you'll have nothing to moan about!'

The telephone rang.

'Wally, answer that phone – and mind that tin of sump oil, you clumsy boy!'

'Hello?' said Wally, just missing the sump oil and picking up the phone.

'Hello. Is that Wally?'

'Yes,' said Wally.

'Well, it's April Phoole here, Wally – you know, YOUR COUSIN!'

Wally Pratt does indeed have a cousin called April Phoole. She is a small, peaches-and-cream sort of girl who lives life with lots of gusto. If she says she's going to do something, she usually does it, whatever the consequences.

When Wally heard that it was April on the phone his eyes rolled up towards the ceiling. He knew that it could mean that she wanted to come and stay. Last time she had come to stay it had led to a full-scale fight in a television studio.

'Can I speak to Aunt Vera, please, Wally?' said the phone.

'Hang on. I'll get her.' Wally beckoned his mother to the telephone.

She put down her adjustable spanner, wiped her oily hands on her pinny and took the handset. 'Hello, April dear! What can I do for you?'

'Please could I come and stay, Aunty?'

Wally overheard this and grimaced as if he'd trodden in something nasty.

'I have taken up horse-racing now, and my horse, Angel Pie, is entered in the last race in the point-to-point at the end of the week. Can I come? It would only take me a morning to ride over to you. Please let me – it could be my lucky break into big-time racing!'

'But where are we going to put the horse? We'll never get it in the kitchen – it's full of bits of motorbike.' Wally's mother sounded very concerned.

'Oh, don't worry about that. I'll just tether him in the recreation field opposite your house. I'll take food out to him – I give him oats in a bucket anyway, and if he wants a drink, he can always use the duck pond.'

Mrs Pratt saw nothing wrong with April's suggestions. 'Very well, April, ride over any time you like!'

She put the phone down. 'Come on, Wally, give me a hand with this blooming side-car. April is coming to stay for the point-to-point, so we may well need a bit of transport. She says it's going to be her lucky break into horse-racing.'

'Huh!' said Wally Pratt indignantly. 'Last time she was going to have a lucky break it was into show business and I nearly ended up with broken legs!'

'Now, don't make a fuss. You've got nothing to worry about. What about me? I've got hardly any money left and now I've got to feed a ravenous niece as well as you.'

There was a rattling sound at the front door.

'That will be the evening paper, Wally. Go and fetch it for me.'

Wally picked the evening paper up from the mat and brought it through to his mother, who glanced at it.

In large print on the back page was an advert that immediately caught her eye and imagination:

WANTED

A THOROUGHLY RELIABLE, TRUSTWORTHY CHAUFFEUR FOR LOCAL BISHOP

QUITE GOOD PAY

WOULD SUIT SOMEONE WITH MECHANICAL SKILLS

3

Captain Smoothy-Smythe

In his office, down at the ABC Garage, Captain Smoothy-Smythe was pouring himself a mid-morning glass of gin.

The Captain isn't really a captain at all. He thinks he looks like one, with smart suede shoes, check trousers and a blue blazer with brass buttons, but he has never been in either the army or the navy, and the only thing he was ever captain of was a school football team, and that wasn't for very long.

He has quite a distinctive way of speaking, and is inclined to call people 'old boy' or even 'old bean'.

The most important thing to know about Captain Smoothy-Smythe is that he is not what he appears to be: he is a con man, and is much more successful and dangerous than someone like Dud Cheque.

The Captain owns the ABC Garage. He is well aware, however, that to be a successful small-time crook and deceiver, you need to be able to think up new things to do. 'Always be on the look-out for a lucky break, old boy!' he used to say.

Running the ABC Garage was very easy for Captain Smoothy-Smythe; he could have done it standing on his head. Admittedly, he did have the occasional brainwave – for instance, he had recently suggested to one of his mechanics that he should go up to the Bishop's Palace and pinch the old boy's petrol back out of his tank – but in general there was very little for the Captain to get his criminal mind working on.

He didn't sit in his office for very long because it was too boring; he got up and decided to go on one of his famous tours of inspection in the workshop. This was at the back of the garage. In its dark and oily interior all sorts of repairs were done to cars, though whether the cars were ever the same after having been in the garage's care, I wouldn't like to say.

'How's it going, men?' the Captain said to his two mechanics, Slimey and Grimey O'Reilly. They were brothers. He always spoke to them as if he was an officer and they were very inferior soldiers.

'It's going OK, sir, thanks,' said Grimey O'Reilly.

'We're just taking the nice new engine out of this little old man's Mini and putting in that old Mini engine we had in the van out the back,' explained Slimey.

'That's it, chaps,' said their lord and master. 'Keep up the good work!'

'I had a spot of bad luck up at the Bishop's yesterday morning,' said Slimey.

'SPOT OF BAD LUCK!' said the Captain angrily. It didn't take very much to make him angry.

'Yer,' said Slimey. 'He rumbled me. Sent me packing.'

'That's *all* I need, BUMBOIL!' said the Captain. 'My profits go haywire if I don't sell at least *some* of the petrol twice! It was one of my best schemes! He used to get driven down here to fill up, we'd flog him a tankful, then we'd go and nick it back and he'd be back down here again for another load . . . Oh well . . . I hope to heck something profitable turns up soon!'

He went back to his boring office. He sat down at his large desk and put his feet up on it. He put his hands behind his head and stared at the ceiling.

An inventive and artful man like Captain Smoothy-Smythe cannot live by selling petrol and repairing cars alone. He desperately needed a profitable scheme or plot in order to put a spring back into his step.

But he couldn't think of one.

He decided to while away the rest of the morning by reading his *Sporting Life*, all about horse-racing.

He looked down the lists of runners and riders at a couple of big meetings, made a selection and lifted the phone to Honest Bert at the betting shop in the town.

'Hello,' he said. 'I want ten quid on Spotty Lad in the 3.30 at Stratford.'

Before he could say anything else, the voice on the other end said, ''Allo, boss!'

'Hey, I jolly well know that voice!' said the Captain.

'Yeah, I should think you does!' said the voice.

'That's Cheque, isn't it? Jolly old Dud Cheque!'

'That's right, boss!' said Dud Cheque, for indeed it was him.

'I haven't seen you since that slight scuffle at the TV studio!' said the Captain. 'What have you been doing to keep yourself in mischief?'

'Well,' said Dud. 'I had to lie low for a while, and then I did nearly a whole day's work up at the Bishop's.'

'Oh, I hear my man Slimey O'Reilly came a bit of a cropper there yesterday,' said the Captain.

'That's right. I come a cropper an' all!'

'I'm sorry to hear that, Cheque, old bean, but why have you answered the phone at Honest Bert's?'

'Well, I've just started working here this morning. Honest Bert is going to be very busy for the

point-to-point and he knows that I know a thing or two about horses, because when we was in Borstal together we used to work on farms and things like that. So I'm helping out in the betting shop,' said Dud.

'Are you? Helping out in the betting shop, eh? I see.' And the Captain's crafty mind started to go into overdrive. 'Cheque,' he said, 'I think it might be a good idea if we met some time very soon to discuss this point-to-point. Would you care to pop over to the garage tomorrow night at about six? We could have a spot of gin, jolly old gin.'

And the Captain put the phone down.

4

Mrs Pratt Meets the Bishop

The deafening roar of a mighty engine split the morning air, and Mrs Vera Pratt turned her motorbike into the drive of the Bishop's Palace. Wally, her son, sat beside her, in the new side-car.

With a screech of finely adjusted brakes and flying gravel, she brought the bike to a spectacular halt outside the front door.

Moments later, the Bishop's Lady Wife was showing Mrs Pratt and Wally into the Bishop's study.

'A Mrs Pratt and her son to see you, Lord Bishop,' she said in her haughtiest voice. She did not approve of Vera's black-leather jacket with the words 'HOUSEWIVES RULE OK?' written on the back in metal studs.

'Ah . . . Good morning, Mrs Pratt. What can I do for you?'

'I've come about the advert in the paper for a chauffeur.'

'Good gracious!' said the Bishop. Somehow Wally's mother wasn't quite what he had had in mind. 'Well, let us have a talk about it, Mrs Pratt . . . Please sit down.' He smiled at her.

'Thank you, Bish!' said Vera Pratt. 'I'll park my backside in this chair. Wally, sit there and be quiet.' She sat down in front of the Bishop's desk, and put her crash-helmet on the floor at her feet.

'And who is this, pray?' said the Bishop pleasantly, pointing towards Wally.

'Oh, that's my lad, Wally. I like to bring him with me when I'm out on the bike – he's very good ballast in the side-car. Nice and heavy.'

'Oh . . . I see.' The Bishop could tell that Mrs Pratt was a rather unusual lady.

'He won't give you any trouble, Bishop. He's very docile, so long as he's not roused.'

Once more her comments about Wally Pratt were accurate. Wally doesn't throw his weight about unless something upsets him. He is, however, very strong and can move quickly if he really has to. His usual tactic when someone annoys him is to get them down and sit on their head before they can say Jack Robinson, or 'Sorry, Wally.'

'Well, now,' said the Bishop. 'I am looking for a chauffeur who will drive me around in my car and look after it. I need someone very reliable, and good with their hands. I'm afraid I had a very unfortunate experience recently with someone who turned out to be dishonest. Are you trustworthy?'

'You bet I am, Bish! I'm as straight as a die! I've had a bit of bother of my own with villains recently, so I know how you feel!'

'And are you good with cars?'

'Of course I am, but I've grown out of them. There's only one way to travel in style these days, Bishop! Motorbike and side-car! Get the wind in your face, smell the hot oil as it swirls round your big end! You can't beat it, I promise you.'

'Are you suggesting,' exclaimed the Bishop, 'that I should give up my car and travel by motor-bicycle?'

'YES!' said Vera Pratt firmly. 'For a start, they are far cheaper than cars. And you look as if you're nice and heavy. You'll make excellent ballast in the side-car – just as good as my Wally!'

'I suppose you might be right. I must say, it does sound rather exciting!' If you are a bishop, you don't have a lot of fun. His eyes began to sparkle at the whole idea of it. 'Very well, Mrs Pratt. You can have the job. Start tomorrow morning!'

'Thanks, Bish. You can rely on me.'

She and Wally left the Palace and went home.

When they got there, they found April Phoole and her horse standing on the doorstep.

Vera Pratt parked the motorbike and side-car and

greeted her niece. 'April, my dear! Come on in and have a nice cup of tea.'

'I must feed Angel Pie first, Aunty. He always has a bucket of oats at about this time – I've brought plenty with me.'

'Oh, do that afterwards! Wally will help you.'

Mrs Pratt took a look at the horse. It seemed very big, especially when compared with April. It was dapple-grey, with a nice white mane. 'I don't actually like horses much, April – you can't take

them apart when they go wrong – but I must say he does look in very good nick. Has he passed his MOT?'

'He is the most blissful horse in all the world!' said April, adoringly.

After tea there was a knock at the door. Wally went to answer it and there on the step stood three friends of his, Bean Pole, Bill Stickers and Ginger Tom.

Bean Pole is tall and thin, which is probably why he is always known as Bean Pole. He is, in many ways, the opposite of Wally, because he is quick and eager.

Bill Stickers is really called Bill Stukely, but got the nickname Bill Stickers when friends in his class saw a notice saying 'BILL STICKERS WILL BE PROSECUTED'. His shirt never stays tucked in, and his mother spends a lot of time telling him he looks a mess.

Ginger Tom is not a cat: he is a small boy called Tom who has ginger hair and freckles.

'Are you coming out, Wally?' said Bean Pole.

'Well, I can't yet really,' said Wally. 'April has come to stay, and before I do anything else, I've got to go and help her get her horse sorted out for the night. There it is over there.' He nodded towards Angel Pie, who was standing near the front gate.

'We'll help!' said Bean Pole.

So the four boys, supervised by April Phoole, got Angel Pie sorted out. They hammered an iron peg into the ground near the duck pond, and April tied one end of a rope to his bridle and the other end to the top of the peg. Then she gave him a huge bucket of oats.

'Cor! He doesn't half eat a lot of oats!' said Bean Pole to her as they watched him have his tea.

'Yes, he does. There's a reason for that,' said April, and she went indoors to read her book, *Horse Racing for Beginners*.

The boys finished the day with a quick game of football on the recreation field.

5

Dud Cheque Meets the Captain

Down at the ABC Garage the next evening, Captain Smoothy-Smythe was brooding. In a few minutes his old partner in crime, Dud Cheque, would show up.

With Dud now working at Honest Bert's betting shop, it should be possible to make a bit of extra profit from some sort of betting scheme at the point-to-point. All the Captain had to do was think of something.

Sometimes, if you want a good idea, it's best not to think too hard about it. Do you remember Archimedes? He was an ancient Greek who had a good idea when he was getting into his bath, and he shouted 'Eureka!', which is more or less ancient Greek for 'Yippee! I've cracked it!' The point is that he wasn't sitting in his study, thinking; he was having a bath, and the water, overflowing, suggested the solution to his problem.

Captain Smoothy-Smythe decided to work on

the same principle, and so, instead of sitting in his office getting more and more stuck, he went on another of his tours of inspection in the workshop. It also gave him a chance to see what Slimey and Grimey O'Reilly were up to.

When he found them, they were busy spraying blue paint on to a car that had once been red.

'Now then, men,' said the Captain, addressing his trusty troops, 'what little trick are you up to this evening?'

'Well, it's like this,' said Grimey. 'We just happen to have heard that the police are going round garages asking about a red Cortina with the same number-plates as this one!'

The Captain suddenly began to feel rather hot: he didn't like visits from the police.

'So,' said Slimey, 'we thought we'd better change its colour rather quick. We'll change the number-plates as well, and make it look like a different car in no time.'

'Good work, men. I'm glad to see that you're getting the hang of the basic skills of car-dealing!' The Captain liked mechanics who could think for themselves. 'Carry on then, chaps! Keep up the good work!' he said, and he wandered out of the workshop and round on to the garage forecourt.

They're disguising one car to look like another, are they? said the Captain to himself, as he looked down the road to see if there was any sign of Dud Cheque.

Then the Archimedes principle struck him. 'Eureka!' he shouted. 'E U - J O L L Y - O L D - R E K - A!'

At that very moment Dud Cheque came into view. He was coming down the steep hill towards the garage on a rusty old bicycle. It would seem that the old bicycle had no brakes because it didn't stop

until it hit the blazered front of Captain Smoothy-Smythe. He and Dud Cheque fell in a tangled heap on to the grass in front of the garage.

'Evening, guv!' said Dud, as they crashed to the ground.

The Captain said something very rude that we can't print here, but Dud knew what it meant.

When the Captain had dusted himself down, and collected his wits, he suggested that they should go into his office for 'a bit of a chat'.

Dud had been in the Captain's office many times before because when he worked at the garage he was often summoned into it and threatened with the sack.

This evening, however, the Captain was hoping to cash in on the fact that Dud worked at Honest Bert's betting shop, so he was going to be nice to him. He would give him some gin, and pretend to be friendly, even if Dud had begun the evening's meeting by running into him at thirty miles an hour, and getting dust and dirt all over his best blazer.

'Cheque, old bean! Absolutely splendid to see you again. How are you, my dear fellow?' oiled the Captain when they were indoors.

'Mustn't complain, ta,' said Dud Cheque.

'That's it!' said the Captain, reluctantly patting the grubby shoulder of Cheque's jacket. 'Let's have a gin, and you can tell me more about what you've been up to since we last met.'

After some talk of this and that, the Captain steered the conversation round to the major topic on his wicked mind. 'So now you're working at Honest Bert's betting shop, are you?'

'Yeah, guv, I just do the odd jobs, like taking bets at the counter, and putting the money in the till.'

The Captain's eyes sparkled at the thought of it. 'And are you expecting to be pretty busy for the point-to-point?' he asked.

'Not half! We open the shop early on the day before races, and on the day itself we set up a betting stall in the race field. We'll have a very busy day! Bert reckons he'll be taking more bets than ever this year.'

'I see,' said Captain Smoothy-Smythe thoughtfully. 'Would you like another gin, old boy?'

'Not half!' said Dud again. He didn't often get offered glasses of gin.

'Cheque,' said the Captain, as he handed Dud a second glass, 'might you be interested, old fellow, in some sort of scheme or other, that might, well . . . be to our advantage, if you see what I mean? Our *mutual* advantage?'

Dud Cheque thought for a short time. 'You mean we could make a bit of money?'

'Exactly!' said the Captain. 'Ex-jolly-old-actly!'

'Whatcher got in mind?' said Dud, holding out his empty glass towards the Captain.

'Let me test your understanding of the betting game, Dud, and see if you come to the same conclusions as I do.' The Captain handed him a refilled glass.

'What horse is the favourite for the big race, the 4.30 – the final race of the afternoon?'

'That's easy!' said Dud. 'Dirty Beast. Everyone knows that. It should win by a mile, especially with Twisty Turner as the jockey.'

'So a lot of people will put money on Twisty Turner and Dirty Beast,' said the Captain.

'Yeah – and the only person who won't win very much is Honest Bert. He'll have to pay out thousands!'

'Right!' said the Captain. 'What would happen if Dirty Beast and Twisty Turner didn't win? *What if an outsider won instead?*'

'Honest Bert would make a fortune – he'd need a dumper-truck to bring all his loot back from the races!' said Dud.

Then he shrugged his thin, miserable shoulders. 'But it won't happen, guv: Twisty'll win it by a mile!'

'Hang on, Dud, old bean!' said the Captain, picking up the gin bottle again. 'I think we could perhaps arrange it so that Dirty Beast comes a bit of a cropper!'

'What! Nobble the horse?' said Dud. 'Don't be daft, boss. They have tests to stop horses being doped these days, and Twisty Turner and the owner will be watching like hawks! It would be like trying to rob the Bank of England!'

'Cheque, my friend,' said the Captain calmly, 'I don't intend to "nobble the horse", as you put it, or rob the Bank of England. What I suggest is simple. I propose that we kidnap Dirty Beast before the race starts, and that we enter another horse, which is identical in appearance but couldn't win a race if it was the only horse in it! The public will put all their money on the horse they *think* is Dirty Beast and, when it doesn't win, they won't come back to Honest Bert to collect any winnings!'

'But all that will happen then, is that Honest Bert will make a lot of money!' interrupted Dud Cheque.

'No he won't,' said the Captain, 'because, as you have already said, *you* will be taking in the money from the public, and there will be so much of it, that if most of it finds its way into the back of my van while the race is on, and people aren't looking, dear old Honest Bert will never even miss it! The main point is that the public won't be asking for it back.'

'Cor . . .' said Dud, who was beginning to get the picture.

'Hang on though,' he said. 'What about Twisty Turner? He'll soon know he's not riding Dirty Beast!'

'My dear chap, nothing could be easier than coping with that little problem. We kidnap him as well, and substitute another jockey in his place. In those bright-coloured clothes and goggles, it shouldn't be too difficult to fool the public. Slimey O'Reilly should perform that task excellently!'

'Blimey, guv – you've thought of everything!' said Dud.

'Thank you, Cheque,' said the Captain, standing up, indicating that the interview, and the free gin, were now at an end.

'Just one little point before you go,' he said, as he showed Dud Cheque to the door. 'If you mention this little wheeze of mine to anyone, you do realize that I would be obliged to break your miserable, scruffy little neck, don't you?'

'Oh yes, guv,' replied Dud. 'Don't worry about that – I can take a hint.'

Dud remounted his bike and rode off, wobbling into the sunset.

6

Vera Pratt's First Day at Work

Mrs Pratt arrived, bright and early, for her first day's work at the Bishop's Palace.

She parked the motorbike and side-car on the gravel drive outside the front door and rang the bell. It was answered by the Bishop's Lady Wife, who

looked down her nose at Mrs Pratt, like a giraffe that thinks it's smelt something unpleasant.

'Yes?' said Lady Wife.

'Morning. I've come to drive the Bish around. I'm reporting for duty!' said Mrs Pratt cheerfully through the hole in the front of her crash-helmet.

'I see. Follow me, if you please.' Lady Wife was more convinced than ever that a driver was an unnecessary extravagance.

She walked elegantly towards the Bishop's study door, and Mrs Pratt followed.

'Mrs Pratt to see you, Lord Bishop,' said Lady Wife, announcing the new driver in a snooty tone. Then she swept off, leaving Vera alone with her new employer.

'Ah . . . Splendid!' said the Bishop in a kindly voice. 'This morning I have got to go and see Colonel Thundering-Blunderer, to talk over the arrangements for the point-to-point. You had better get the car out.'

'C A R!' said Mrs Pratt. 'Come off it, Bish! We're not going to travel round in a poncy old car. Re-member? We're going to travel cheaply, but in style! By motorbike!'

'Er . . . Oh, yes, you're quite right. How silly of me! Is the . . . er . . . motor . . . er . . . bike all ready?' The Bishop sounded a little nervous.

'You bet!' said Vera. 'I spent all yesterday evening

tuning the twin carbs and hoovering out the side-car. Come on, Bish – let's go!'

And off they set towards Colonel Thundering-Blunderer's farmhouse in a nearby village. The Bishop sat in the side-car, wearing a crash-helmet and a huge black-leather coat that Vera lent him.

Once they were out of the town, Vera opened the throttle wide.

'LEAN OVER ON THE CORNERS,

BISH,' she shouted, 'OR WE MAY GO IN THE DITCH!'

The Lord Bishop did as he was asked, and they tore through the country lanes – lickettysplit! The wind rushed into their faces, and pulled the startled Bishop's cheeks back so that he had an uncontrollable smile on his reverent face.

He had never been so frightened, and excited, in his whole life!

'GO FOR IT, MRS PRATT!' He yelled at the top of his voice.

'YOU BET! HOLD ON, YOUR HOLINESS!' shouted Vera, and she lowered her head and shoulders over the handlebars and clipped the grass on a vicious left-hand bend!

'WHEEEEeeeeeeeee!' they shouted together.

Before very long they arrived at the farmhouse. The Bishop, with shaking legs, got out of the side-car and went inside for a discussion with Colonel Thundering-Blunderer about the details of the prize-giving for the point-to-point.

Vera and the motorbike and side-car waited out of sight, round the side of the stables, until they had finished.

Then they were off down the road again.

'I MUST SAY,' shouted the Bishop, 'THIS IS CERTAINLY A MOST INVIGORATING MEANS OF TRANSPORT!'

'OF COURSE IT IS!' Vera called back, as they took off into the air over a small, humpbacked bridge. 'IT WILL DO YOU A POWER OF GOOD, BISH. IT WILL MAKE YOU MORE UP-TO-DATE AND MODERN!'

The Bishop became thoughtful when he heard this. Perhaps his new driver was absolutely right. He had become a bit stuck in his ways recently, and maybe a bit of modernization would do him good.

He was still rather worried that he didn't know much about horse-racing, or what to say to jockeys when he gave them their cups and prizes. Perhaps Mrs Pratt would be able to give him some advice.

These thoughts filled his head as Vera steered the motorbike and side-car back through the country lanes with amazing speed and skill. She cut every corner, narrowly missed a farm dog that ran out at them, flew under some level-crossing gates just before they closed, and sent an elderly lollipop lady, at a school on the edge of town, running for cover behind her children.

When they got indoors again the Bishop invited Vera to join him in his study.

'I have been thinking about how I need to become more modern,' he said to her. 'I am particularly worried about this point-to-point. You seem to me to be a very modern lady, I wondered if you could tell me anything about horse-racing and betting!'

'That would be a cinch!' said Vera. 'Mind if park my butt?'

'Pardon?'

'Mind if I sit down?'

'No, no, not at all,' said the Bishop.

'Right. Betting is pretty simple. The *favourite* is the horse that most people think will win, and an outsider is a horse that is not very likely to win, but if it does, and you have bet on it, you make a lot – maybe as much as a hundred to one!'

'What does that mean?'

'It means, Bish, that if you put a pound on it and it won, you would win a hundred pounds!'

'Good gracious,' said the Bishop, and his mouth opened with amazement. 'I say! A hundred pounds!' His round face lit up with delight at the very idea.

'Does that give you some idea?' asked Vera.

'It certainly gives me *lots* of ideas!' said the Bishop.

'Well, that's good . . . Actually, talking of money,' said Vera a little timidly, 'I would be grateful if you could let me have some money now for petrol for the bike.'

'Yes,' said the Bishop, 'that is a very reasonable request. How much should we get?'

'Ten pounds would go quite a long way,' said Vera.

The Bishop gave her two five-pound notes. Vera Pratt got up and left the room, and went outside to polish the motorbike.

'I say!' said the Bishop to himself in his empty study. 'Think of winning a hundred pounds!'

The Bishop's mind was in a whirl: the more he thought about it, the more he felt that a few pounds invested on a horse or two would do no harm at all: why can't a bishop have a bit of fun, after all?

7

Vera Pratt's Second Day at Work

When Wally's mother arrived for work the next morning, the Bishop had a surprise for her.

'Good morning, Mrs Pratt,' he said.

'Good morning, Bish,' said Mrs Pratt. She had been up early and had polished the bike until it shone. She was looking forward to her second day at work. 'Where are we going to bomb off to today?'

'We have got a few trips to make this morning,' replied her employer. 'But first, because it is the point-to-point tomorrow, I would be grateful if you would convey me to Honest Bert's betting shop.'

Vera could hardly believe her ears!

'Only *you* must know that that's where I am going,' whispered the Bishop. 'Get the bike started, and wait for me out at the front.'

Vera Pratt did as she was told. She made sure that the cushions in the side-car were nice and neat, then she pulled on her black-leather gauntlets and bright red crash-helmet and kicked the mighty engine into life.

The deep roar of the huge bike was music to her ears!

She sat astride the massive petrol tank and waited. Before very long, an elderly woman appeared from round the side of the Bishop's Palace. She was wearing an old green coat and a headscarf. Her legs were encased in wrinkled brown stockings and she had bedroom slippers on her feet.

She was carrying a large, plastic shopping-bag, and she swayed from side to side as she waddled across the drive towards Vera.

'Would you like a lift to town with us, ducks? I'm sure His Lordship, the Bishop, wouldn't mind,' said Vera in a kindly voice.

'I *A M His Lordship the Bishop*!' said the old lady in a whisper.

And so it was! He had even put a squiggly line of lipstick across his mouth, and powder on his cheeks.

'O H! That's very clever of you, Your Lordship: you don't look at all like a bishop now!'

'That's exactly my plan, Mrs Pratt. I intend to put a bet or two on at Honest Bert's, and then I'll come back here to change, before going off to visit some of the ill people in the parish. My wife has been

complaining a lot recently about not having enough money for the housekeeping. Some winnings would come in very handy!'

The Bishop got into the side-car and put a crash-helmet on top of his headscarf.

With a roar, they were off down the road.

'I'll take it easy on the bends today, Bish, so there's no need to lean out – I don't think it would be appropriate with you dressed like that!' shouted Vera, above the throbbing engine.

The Bishop gave her a thumbs-up sign from the side-car.

In a trice they were outside Honest Bert's betting shop.

'Wait for me here then, please,' said the Bishop, pulling the plastic shopping-bag out from the depths of the side-car. Then, taking his courage in both hands, he waddled across the road and through the door of Honest Bert's establishment.

Have you ever been inside a betting shop?

Neither have I.

Neither had the Bishop.

He felt very nervous, mainly, of course, because he didn't want to be recognized, but also because he didn't know what to do!

The betting shop was full of men, and smoke. Commentaries of horse races were coming from a loudspeaker in the corner.

Along one wall there were several blackboards, with lists of horses on them and numbers after their names, and some of the men seemed very busy looking at them. Others were studying their newspapers.

The Bishop pushed back the rim of his headscarf and looked round to see if there was anything that referred to the next day's point-to-point.

His heart, deep beneath the old green overcoat, was beating fast!

After a worrying few moments, he saw it. At the top end of the room, very near a counter with two grilles in it, that reminded the Bishop of a bank, was a section of blackboard headed:

'Point-To-Point – Runners and Riders'

The Bishop went up to it, remembering to walk like an old lady with bad feet – which wasn't easy to do in his present, nervous state.

He looked at the bottom of the board for the 4.30 – the last race of the day. There it was – a list of horses and their jockeys. The very last line on the board gave him a nasty start:

FOLLOWING THIS RACE THE PRIZES WILL BE GIVEN OUT BY THE LORD BISHOP

His powdered face blushed a little. He scanned the list: Proper Charlie, Teacher's Pet, Prunes and Custard, Angel Pie, Tooti Fruiti. Then he saw what he was after: Dirty Beast (Favourite).

'Right,' he said to himself. 'If I want to win

money, I should obviously put some on the favourite – after all, he's the most likely to win. Why else would he be called the favourite?'

Men were forming small queues at the two grilles and were paying money in, over the counter.

The Bishop shuffled into the shortest queue and rehearsed to himself what he was going to say, 'Good morning, I hope that the favourite wins the 4.30 race at the point-to-point, so I would like to put five pounds on Dirty Beast, please.'

He watched apprehensively as the men in front of him paid their money and left the shop. Soon it was his turn.

He stood in front of the grille and leaned forward slightly towards it. Then, trying hard to speak like an old lady with bad feet, he said: 'Good morning, I . . . er . . . hope that the best horse wins . . . I mean the favourite. Please put this . . . er, five pounds on Birty Deast . . . No, I mean Dirty Beast.'

The voice behind the grille spoke: ''ALLO, BISHOP!' it said.

The voice belonged to Dud Cheque.

The shock of being recognized caused the Bishop's mouth to fall open in horror! And then a very unfortunate thing happened.

His false teeth fell out. They clattered down his green overcoat and on to the counter, where they lay for an instant, pink and white, in the glare of the betting shop's bright neon lighting.

Dud Cheque's hand came out under the grille, like a lizard's tongue when it's spotted something tasty, and he swept the teeth, still warm, into his pocket. It was all the evidence he'd need for getting his own back on the Bishop!

The Bishop dropped his shopping-bag, turned and rushed from the shop in startled, toothless terror.

8

The Bishop's Disharshter!

He forgot all about pretending to be an old lady with bad feet as he crossed the road to the motorbike and side-car. He ran as fast as his bedroom slippers could carry him.

When he got to the bike, Mrs Pratt was not there!

In desperation, he jumped into the side-car and ducked down as low as he could inside it.

When something terrible happens to you, do you go as red as a beetroot?

So do I.

So did the Bishop.

He pulled the headscarf over his blushing cheeks, crouched down as low as he could, and wished the road would open up and swallow him. He also wondered where Mrs Pratt had got to.

But a moment later she arrived: the Bishop thought he saw her come from a door at the side of the betting shop, but he may have been wrong – the embarrassment of being spotted and losing his teeth in Honest Bert's may have confused him.

'You didn't take very long to place your bets, Bish!' said Vera in a jaunty voice. 'Sorry I wasn't here, I had a little business to do.'

'MISHES PWATT,' said the Bishop, 'THERE HASH BEEN AN ASHOLUTE CATASHTWOPHY! A DISHARSHTER!'

Mrs Pratt's mouth opened in amazement. (But no teeth fell out.)

'I'VE LOSHT MY TEEF!'

'Losht your teef!?' repeated Vera. 'Where?'

'In ver betting shop, of coursh!' said the Bishop. 'And ver garshly little man behind ver counter recognized me, and took vem!'

'Right!' said Vera. 'Let's get out of here!'

With a kick like an angry mule, she brought the

mighty engine to life and in moments they were on their way.

Vera steered the bike out of town. She went very fast and, because the Bishop was far too upset to think about leaning properly on the corners, they nearly went into several ditches. On right-hand bends, the side-car wheel lifted into the air.

It was the least of the Bishop's worries.

Vera parked in a quiet gateway so that they could have a discussion and think of what to do.

'Oh, Mishes Pwatt,' said the Bishop in the silence as the engine stopped. 'Whatever am I going to do?'

Vera had never seen a Bishop, dressed as an old lady, burst into tears, but she thought she might be going to now.

'Ver point-to-point ish tomowwow! I've got to give out ver pwyshes! I'll never get a shpare pair of teef in vat time! My wife will find out vat I've been in a betting shop! And what about ver garshly little man behind ver counter?'

'Yes,' said Vera calmly, 'he'll probably try to blackmail you.'

'WHAT!' said the Bishop. He had now gone very pale.

'Well, if he's got a criminal mind, he'll probably look on the teeth as something he's kidnapped. He'll demand money as a ransom for them.'

'*He'sh got a cwiminal mind all wight*! He'sh ver man

who was my chauffeur! I caught him twying to steal my petrol! I gave him ver sack!'

'In that case, you certainly are in trouble. He will want revenge and he knows you'll want it kept quiet that you went into a betting shop. It has all the ingredients of a classic five-figure kidnap.'

'What dush a five-figure kidnap mean?'

'It means he'll demand several thousand pounds from you – ten at least.'

The Bishop's toothless mouth fell open again, and he went even paler. He said something not very bishop-like under his breath, but we can't print it here.

'There may just be one way out,' said Vera quietly.

'What?'

'Well, I could drop you back at the Palace and go home and get my large adjustable spanner. I could then go back down to the betting shop with it and wait by the side door until he comes out. When he does, I could smash him under the chin with it, and pinch your teeth back.'

'I shay!' said the Bishop. 'What a shimply shooper idea!'

'What does he look like?'

'Like a wat.'

'A what?' said Vera.

'A wat – you know, like a large mouse.'

So Vera Pratt went into action. She dropped the Bishop off, and went home for the spanner, which she tucked under her leather biker's jacket.

Then she stationed herself in the alleyway at the side of Honest Bert's and waited for the member of staff the Bishop had described to her to come out.

She waited a long time.

It would not really have mattered how long she had waited because there was a fault in her plan.

Dud Cheque was no longer there, he was now down at the ABC Garage, receiving instructions from his lord and master in crime, Captain Smoothy-Smythe.

9

The Captain Goes Into Action

'Right, men!' said Captain Smoothy-Smythe to Dud and the O'Reilly brothers. 'The point-to-point is tomorrow, so it's time we got ourselves a horse. We want one that looks exactly the same as Dirty Beast – chestnut with a white flash down its forehead.'

'That's easy, boss!' said Grimey. 'The best horse-dealer round here is Shady Wood. He's bound to have one.'

'SHADY WOOD! Who on earth is Shady Wood? He sounds like an absolute rotter!'

'Oh no, sir,' said Slimey, 'He's a real expert on horses. He lives in a caravan on the edge of the road at Old Codgers Farm. He owns all the horses and ponies in the fields there.'

'Right!' said the Captain. 'Get in the van and go and see him. Dud, as you know so much about horses from your Borstal days down on the farm, you'd better be in charge. I'll stay here and get a stable ready in the workshop.'

'What about cash, guv?' said Dud Cheque. 'We'll need money before Shady will part with a horse.'

'Here's a hundred pounds. Don't spend it all. After all, you're only trying to buy a horse that couldn't win a race in a month of Sundays! Fifty quid should do it!'

'OK, boss,' said Dud, and he and the two brothers climbed into the van.

Half an hour later the three of them were standing next to Mr Shady Wood, looking over a gate at a field of very decrepit horses.

'Look, Shady,' said Dud. 'We have a special need for a chestnut horse with a white flash down its forehead, which couldn't win a horse race in a month of Sundays. Never mind why.'

'Ooo Arrr,' said Shady Wood, chewing a piece of straw. 'That bain't be no problem, squire.'

'Good!' said Grimey. 'What are you going to recommend then?'

'Oi got 'undreds of 'osses that'll suit yer! Hows abart that 'un over yonder by the 'edge?'

Shady Wood pointed to a large brown horse on the far side of the field. It was lying down eating grass, and certainly did look very like Dirty Beast to the untrained eye.

'I think he's right, Dud,' said Grimey. 'The colour's right, and the size.'

'Ee's a proper beauty, that 'oss!' said Shady Wood. ''Ee won't win no races, but 'ee don't look too bad.'

'What's his name, Shady?' asked Slimey.

''Ee's called Trigger. I reckon 'ee'll do the trick for yer!'

'Are you sure about him, Dud?' said Slimey O'Reilly. 'He doesn't look very active, lying there like that.'

'Don't be a twit!' replied Dud. 'We don't want a horse that goes and wins – or we'll have to give all the money back to the public in winnings! He looks as if he'll be good for a couple of fences, and then he'll slip to the back of the field. Everyone will just think that Dirty Beast has had a bad day.'

''Ee'll slip ter the back o' the field all right!' said Shady Wood. ''Ow much was you thinking of paying?'

'What would you say to fifty pounds?' said Dud Cheque.

'I'd say "not enough",' said Shady.

'OK, a hundred pounds and not a penny more, and no questions asked,' said Dud, handing over the Captain's money.

'Ooo Arrr,' said Shady. 'You go back to yer garidge, and I'll bring 'im round after dark. That's what I usually does when I'm deliverin' 'osses.'

Dud led the two O'Reilly brothers back to the

van with a grin on his face. Everything seemed to be going very well.

Mr Shady Wood also had a grin on his face, later that evening, when he drew up outside the ABC Garage with his tractor and horse-trailer.

'Right! Come on, men!' said the Captain to Dud and the O'Reilly brothers. 'Get the animal unloaded and into the workshop before anyone spots us!'

Between them they undid the back of the trailer. Captain Smoothy-Smythe stood back and watched them – he had had a very busy afternoon getting the stable area ready, and felt that he had done his fair share of hard work for the day.

While they all kept a look-out, Shady Wood led the horse through the workshop doors. The moment it got inside it slumped down on the straw behind a written-off Morris Minor.

'I say, Cheque, the old blighter doesn't seem very active!' spluttered the Captain as they all studied the horse. 'We don't want it to be a complete no-hoper or we'll be rumbled! What's it called?'

'Trigger,' said Dud Cheque and Shady Wood together.

'TRIGGER! It looks more like TRIGGER MORTIS!' said the Captain. 'It will be capable of getting round at least *some* of the course, won't it?'

'Ooo Arrr,' said Shady. 'Trigger is very fit. Considering.'

'Considering! Considering what?'

'Good night to yer, squire,' called Shady Wood as he got back on to his tractor and roared away in a cloud of blue smoke.

The Captain was puzzled. He picked up a back bumper that was lying beside the Morris Minor and prodded Trigger on the rump with it.

Slowly, Trigger stood up.

Captain Smoothy-Smythe, Grimey and Slimey O'Reilly and Dud Cheque took a good look at him. The moment they did so, they could see what Shady Wood had meant by 'considering'.

Trigger stood there, wobbling slightly and panting. He only had one back leg.

Dud Solves a Problem

'CHEQUE! YOU DUMBO! YOU PEA-
BRAINED IDIOT!' roared the Captain, turning
red. 'Only you could go out with someone else's
money and come back with a three-legged racehorse! NITFACE! I've a good mind to beat you
over your thick head with the bumper off this rotten
car!'

'Hang on, guv! You told me to get a horse that
couldn't win a race . . .'

'I DIDN'T SAY GET ONE THAT
COULD HARDLY STAND UP! BUM-
BOIL!'

Dud Cheque realized that, once more in his
miserable life, he had made a mistake. It looked as if
he was going to be dismissed yet again. He was
right.

'Get out of my sight before I chop you up into
bite-sized chunks and feed you to this blooming,
half-dead horse!' The Captain was now very red in

the face – a sort of plum colour, and was gritting his teeth and clenching his fists.

'Get me a horse that fits Dirty Beast's description, with FOUR LEGS, by tomorrow morning, or you will owe me one hundred pounds and I shall personally get the cash from you, even if it means taking you apart to find it!'

'OK, boss, keep your hair on,' said Dud Cheque.

'HAIR ON! My hair is on! Yours won't be if you don't find me a Dirty Beast look-alike for the 4.30 tomorrow, because I shall personally scalp you. GET OUTTTTT!'

Dud got out.

He left the ABC Garage and started to walk home.

He hadn't gone very far when he passed the town recreation field. The night was dark, and as he walked he peered over, in the blackness, towards the duck pond. He remembered the afternoon that he and the Captain had ended up sitting in it – but that's another story.

As he looked, something caught his eye. It was a horse, a fine-looking, four-legged horse which, even at this late hour, seemed to be chomping the lush grass that grew on the edge of the football pitch.

Dud went towards it, gingerly. Despite his boasting about his Borstal days down on the farm, he was a little scared of horses. They were much bigger than he was, and didn't seem to care if they butted him in the chest with their heads, or stood on his feet.

'Hello, my beauty,' said Dud in a whisper, trying to make friends with the horse. It didn't answer back.

It was tethered, by a rope, to a metal peg. Dud bent down and pulled the peg upwards out of the ground.

Moments later, Angel Pie, for it was he, was

pulling Dud Cheque through a hedge at the far side of the recreation field. After a struggle, Dud persuaded the animal to change course, and he led it triumphantly back towards the side door of the ABC Garage.

The lights were still on, and from the workshop Dud thought he could hear voices.

He knocked on the door. Slimey O'Reilly opened it.

'Is the guv still here?' said Dud softly.

'No, he's gone to the pub. We've stayed to finish respraying a couple of motors that need to change colour pretty quick. He said he'd be back about midnight to see how we're getting on.'

'Good. Look what I've found, boys!' said Dud, smiling all over his unpleasant little face.

He walked the bewildered Angel Pie into the workshop.

'My troubles are over, lads! The boss told me to get a horse with four legs by tomorrow morning, or he'd chop me up into bite-sized pieces – and look! I've found one!'

Slimey and Grimey looked at Angel Pie. Then Grimey spoke: 'I can still see a slight problem for you, Dud.'

'What?'

'It just so happens that Dirty Beast, the favourite in the 4.30 tomorrow, is a chestnut horse with a white streak down its forehead.'

'Yes,' added Slimey. 'And the horse that you have on that there piece of rope just happens to be grey, with a white mane and black feet!'

Dud Cheque went quiet and stopped smiling. He hadn't thought of that. As you may have realized, he is no genius.

'Wait a minute,' said Grimey, after a moment or two. 'We could spray it!'

'That's right!' said his brother. 'After all, that's what we do when we want to change the colour of a car!'

'Do you have chestnut-coloured car paint?' said Dud, who didn't remember ever having seen a chestnut-coloured car.

'We'll mix some in no time!' exclaimed Slimey. 'Get the horse into the body shop – right away!'

The O'Reilly brothers, expert garage men, got to work!

Grimey mixed the paint, and Slimey did all the preparation work. He got all the dust and dirt off poor Angel Pie's coat and sandpapered his feet, ready for a good, glossy finish.

'Will we need to rust-proof him, do you think?' said Grimey.

'No. We haven't got time. Just a top coat should do it!' replied his brother.

Dud was amazed at their skill.

By a quarter to twelve, a chestnut horse with a

white stripe down its face was standing in the middle of the workshop floor. It was a miracle of modern bodywork.

When the Captain returned from the pub at midnight, he was astounded and delighted.

'My word!' he said. 'My jolly old word. It doesn't look as if I'm going to need to turn you inside out tomorrow after all, Cheque! You really have surprised me! Well done, chaps! Jolly well done!'

He stepped forward to pat the magnificent horse on the neck.

'Don't do that, sir!' exclaimed Slimey. 'He's not quite dry yet!'

This outburst startled the already mystified Angel Pie, who threw back his head, and whinnied. As he did so, the Captain noticed something that sent a shock of horror through him.

'Hang on a minute. Did you see that?'

'See what?' asked Dud.

'When he opened his mouth just then. The blighter hasn't got any front teeth!'

'So what?' said Dud.

'Look, Cheque, you half-wit. Horses are ident- ified by their teeth! Experts at race-meetings are the sort of people who can look into a horse's mouth and tell how old it is, and who its mother was and nonsense like that! I bet the *real* Dirty Beast has got a lovely set of teeth. Where are we going to get a set of teeth for a horse at this time of night? We're done for!'

Dud Cheque started to smile. He reached into his jacket pocket and brought out a magnificent set of false teeth. He held them up for all to see.

They glistened, pink and white, in the sharp, electric lamplight.

The Morning of the Point-to-Point

I don't know if you've ever seen what happens when an eight-year-old girl wakes up on the morning of a point-to-point and looks out of her window to gaze adoringly at the horse of her dreams, who is going to sweep her to victory in the 4.30 race, and he's not there.

It's not a pretty sight.

April Phoole could not believe her eyes. Angel Pie was nowhere to be seen. The recreation field was totally horseless.

Her mouth dropped open, she let out a terrifying scream and her eyes filled with 'where-has-he-gone' tears.

She pulled on her jodhpurs and hacking jacket, and rushed downstairs and out of the front door. She ran across the field to where she had tethered Angel Pie near the pond, the evening before.

Nothing. All she found was the metal peg that she had tied his rope to. It was lying on the grass.

'Aunt Vera,' she said in a determined way when she got back indoors.

'Yes, dear?' Her aunt was sitting next to Wally at the breakfast table.

'There has been a disaster. Angel Pie has slipped his tether and bolted!'

'KNICKER-ELASTIC!' said Mrs Pratt.

'No,' said April, 'it was rope. It's my fault – I can't have tied the knots properly.'

'Bloomin' 'eck,' said Wally. 'What are you going to do now, April?'

'I shall get him back.' She frowned and clenched her fists. She was a very spirited girl. 'He can't have gone very far. I'll scour the countryside for him. He *will* run in the 4.30 this afternoon!'

Down at the ABC Garage, Captain Smoothy-Smythe was also determined that Angel Pie should run in the 4.30 – but disguised as Dirty Beast!

'Well,' said Vera Pratt, 'if you are going to scour the countryside, and I'm going to take the Lord Bishop to the races after lunch, you'd better start right away.'

'I'll phone Bean Pole, Bill and Ginger,' said Wally. 'They'll help.' He went off to telephone his friends, and a few moments later all five of them began their search.

They looked high and low – over hedges, under bridges, in people's back gardens, in the church-yard, in Old Codgers Wood – everywhere.

The only place they didn't look was at the point-to-point field itself!

If they had, they might well have seen Captain Smoothy-Smythe, Dud Cheque and the O'Reilly brothers standing near all the horse-boxes, with their van. Inside the van was a rather fine, but confused, chestnut horse with a white streak down its forehead.

They had arrived at the field early in the morning. The O'Reilly brothers had been working for most of the night on the Bishop's false teeth and, after quite a lot of filing and grinding, and adding bits on with car-body filler, they had got them to fit Angel Pie a treat!

He'd even worn them to eat a bucket of breakfast oats which the O'Reillys had kindly provided.

'Right, chaps,' said the Captain, rubbing his hands together. 'All we have to do now is wait for the horse-box containing Dirty Beast.'

'What do we do then, boss?' asked Dud Cheque, who had just finished helping Honest Bert to put up his betting stall.

'What the blazes do you think we do, Cheque? We locate Twisty Turner and bonk him over the jolly old nut! Idiot!'

'Oh yeah. I get the idea,' said Dud, sheepishly.

'I should hope you do! I sometimes think you don't know the first thing about horse-racing!'

Sure enough, in the middle of the morning, a large horse-box with *Dirty Beast – Everyone's Favourite* painted on its doors pulled into the field.

In the driver's seat was Mr Twisty Turner, the famous jockey. Next to him sat Pete Bogg, the horse's owner.

The horse-box rumbled over the field, lurching from side to side as it crossed the tracks made by other lorries. It stopped near several vehicles which

had brought other horses, and the two men got down from the cab.

'Right, men! Into action!' snarled the Captain under his breath.

The O'Reillys got into the garage van and backed it up close to the rear of Dirty Beast's horse-box, blocking it off from view. The Captain and Dud followed on foot.

Twisty Turner stretched: he had had a long journey. Pete Bogg went to the back of the box and started to undo the huge tailgate, which would form a ramp down which Dirty Beast could walk.

'Ah! The proud owner of none other than Dirty Beast, I presume!' said the Captain, walking up to him.

'Yes?' said Pete Bogg.

'What a lovely day for a point-to-point!'

'Well, so what if it is?' Pete Bogg wanted to get on unloading his horse so that he could give it some exercise. He didn't want to stop and talk to well-dressed idiots! 'Excuse me, mate – I've got work to do.'

'Oh yes, of course – unloading the jolly old horse, what!' While the Captain was making this vain attempt to get the owner talking, Slimey and Grimey O'Reilly and Dud Cheque were approaching Pete from the back. Dud was carrying the starting-handle from the garage van.

'That's right, I'm unloading my horse. Now, do me a favour, mate, push off and leave me in peace.' Pete Bogg put his hands on his hips as he said this, and looked the Captain full in the eye.

Just as he finished speaking, Dud brought the handle down on his head. 'Oooooh!' exclaimed Pete Bogg, as he fell face first in the lush green grass.

'Right, men! Into the cab with him and then we'll give the jolly old jockey the same medicine!' whispered the Captain, excitedly.

They dragged the dazed owner to the passenger door of the horse-box.

The Captain went back to the rear of the

favourite's lorry. Sure enough, moments later Twisty Turner, complete in red-and-yellow silk jockey's outfit, came from the other side to join him.

'Good morning, old boy,' said the Captain, with a broad and welcoming smile.

'Morning,' said Twisty. 'Have you seen the fellow who was opening the back of this horse-box?'

'Can't say I have, old bean.'

'Funny . . . I wonder where he went . . .'

The Captain could see Dud Cheque, with the starting-handle raised high above his head, approaching Twisty from behind, and was just about to start another sentence, to stop the jockey looking round, when he realized he had a problem.

Twisty Turner was wearing a jockey's crash-helmet!

'Err . . . Excuse me, old fellow, but I accuse you of stealing my jockey's helmet – I just saw you do it!'

'Don't talk so daft, you big Nellie!' said Twisty.

'Prove that that helmet is yours, then!' shouted the Captain.

'Look! It's got my blinking name in!' said Twisty, angrily.

He undid the chin-strap and took the helmet off to show the Captain. At that instant, a metal starting-handle descended on his unprotected head, and he, too, sank to the ground.

Dirty Business

Captain Smoothy-Smythe and his three wicked colleagues didn't take very long to do what they had to do.

They dragged the groaning figure of Twisty Turner round to the passenger door of the large horse-box, and the O'Reilly brothers pulled him and the semi-conscious form of Pete Bogg up into the cab.

Dud Cheque and Grimey O'Reilly then got the back doors of the garage van open and coaxed the bewildered Angel Pie out and down some planks on to the grass. Slimey, meanwhile, was in the cab of the horse-box coaxing Twisty Turner out of his silk jockey's outfit!

A few moments later Slimey looked like one of the most experienced point-to-point jockeys the world has ever known. He had a red-and-yellow silk top, bright white breeches, shiny black boots and a matching silk cap covering his racing-helmet.

He tapped the side of his boot with his short whip. He thought he looked great!

He certainly looked better than Twisty Turner at that moment, because Twisty was sitting in the cab of the horse-box in his jockey underpants, with an old blanket round his shoulders!

'Right, chaps!' said the Captain. 'We've still got work to do. I'll look after the horse, you three get in the horse-box and get that horse and those two blighters hidden away before anyone starts asking awkward questions.'

'OK, boss. We'll stick the vehicles in the bushes round the back, and tie these two up in your office, in case they come round,' said Grimey.

'That's it, men!' said the Captain. He was pleased when his troops thought of things for themselves: it put a victorious grin on his face.

'What about this horse, though?' said Dud, pointing to the back of the horse-box with the *real* Dirty Beast still inside it.

'What do you mean "What about this horse"? Just put it in the workshop and lock the jolly old door. We'll deal with it later.'

'But what if someone comes snooping and spots it?' asked Dud.

'Look, Cheque, you dumbo! What do we do to cars if we don't want snooping people to spot them?' growled the Captain.

'We spray 'em a different colour, boss,' said Dud Cheque.

'WELL, SPRAY THE HORSE, THEN – DUNDERHEAD!' shouted the Captain, and, taking the new-look Angel Pie in his coat of chestnut paint by the bridle, he walked off towards the exercise ring.

Dud Cheque and Grimey O'Reilly climbed into the horse-box beside its two unconscious occupants, and Slimey got into the driver's seat.

He started the engine and drove them all down to the nearby A B C Garage.

When they got there, the three of them opened the side door to the workshops and dragged the unfortunate Mr Turner and Mr Bogg through into the Captain's office. While Dud Cheque tied their hands together and trussed them to the legs of the Captain's large desk, the O'Reilly brothers poured the remains of the Captain's gin bottle down the dazed men's throats.

'That should keep them asleep for a nice long time,' said Grimey.

Then they went outside again and lowered the lorry's ramp. They led the magnificent Dirty Beast into the oily interior of the dimly lit garage.

Slimey parked the horse-box out of the way in the bushes at the back of the garage, and then all three surveyed the captured favourite.

'What colour do you think would suit the old fella?' asked Slimey.

'Well,' replied his brother, 'we don't have time to mix anything, so he'd better be the colour of a car paint we've already got.'

'What? You mean like Sirocco Red?' said Dud.

'Of course not Sirocco Red! Who's ever seen a Sirocco Red horse! That would make any snooper suspicious straight away!' said Grimey. 'No, let's

give him a nice new glossy top coat of grey, with a white mane and some nice black hooves! We've got all those colours.'

And that is what they did.

At about the same time as they were doing it, Wally Pratt, April, Bean Pole, Ginger Tom and Bill Stickers were returning empty-handed to Wally's house.

It was midday, and they had given up their search for Angel Pie.

'We couldn't find him, Mum,' said Wally to his mother, who was doing a bit of dusting and polishing.

'Oh-dear-oh-lor,' said his mother. 'Poor little April. Just hang on a moment, Wally, while I finish doing this exhaust system, and then we'll think what to do.'

Very soon the bike's exhaust pipes were shining to her satisfaction, and she put down her cloth.

'Right. Come over here, you lot!' she called, and the five youngsters assembled round the motorbike and side-car.

'I've got a feeling that Angel Pie has been nicked!' said Wally's mum.

'That's right,' said April. 'He wouldn't have gone far on his own. And another thing – he'd have come back of his own accord for his breakfast bucket of oats. You see,' she added rather sheepishly, 'he doesn't have any front teeth, so he needs oats because he can't eat much grass. When he looks as if he's grazing, he's really just sucking the grass. If the robbers don't know that, he could starve!'

'Cor!' said Wally Pratt.

'Well,' said his mother, 'I suggest that Bean Pole, Ginger Tom and Bill Stickers start out for the point-to-point straight away, and keep an eye out for anything suspicious. Wally and April, come with me. I've got to go and get some petrol before I call for the Bishop, and a trip to the A B C Garage will give us a last chance to scour the countryside for the horse.'

So saying, Mrs Vera Pratt went upstairs and changed into her very best red-leather motorbike racing suit.

She joined Wally and April downstairs in the hallway, where she pulled on her leather gauntlets and crash-helmet. 'Let's go, Daddyo!' she said, tucking a duster under her leather belt.

April climbed into the side-car: Wally got on the pillion. Vera kicked the mighty machine into deep-throated life and, with a thunder-cracking roar, they tore off towards the A B C Garage.

When they got there the garage was closed.

'Knicker-elastic!' said Vera.

'Perhaps it's just closed for lunch,' said Wally, which was sensible of him, because it was indeed lunchtime.

'Maybe there will be someone round the back,' said April.

She got out of the side-car and walked towards the back of the garage. Wally joined her.

When they got to the side, they saw the door to the workshop. It was padlocked: they knocked on it but heard no reply.

'Let's look through that window up there,' said Wally.

There were several empty tins of grey car-paint lying around near the door, so they piled a few of them up, and, with Wally helping her, April stood on tiptoe on them and could just reach the grimy pane of glass set high in the workshop door.

What she saw inside the garage took her breath away!

13

That's the Spirit, April

'Quick, Aunt Vera! It's Angel Pie!' shouted April, jumping down from the tins and running to the motorbike. 'Angel Pie is inside the garage! I can see his grey head and white mane behind a lot of bits of broken cars!'

'Right!' said Vera Pratt, woman of action. 'Wally, find some rope or chain or something. We'll have those doors off in no time!'

Wally went round the back of the garage and started searching in piles of scrap-iron for some chain. His mother and April pushed the motorbike and side-car in front of the workshop doors, and when Wally returned with some steel cable that he'd found on the back of an old breakdown truck, they were ready for action!

Vera tied the cable through the padlock on the door and put the other end round the bracket that connected the bike to its huge side-car.

'Wally, get on the pillion, and April, get in the

back seat of the side-car again. We'll need all the weight we can get on the back wheel!'

They did as they were told. The engine flared into life and, with a roar, clouds of smoke, burning rubber and flying grit, the bike ripped the side doors off the garage!

April, her aunt and her cousin rushed into the workshop. She went to pat and kiss the horse, as any small girl who's just found her lost horse would.

The horse threw back its head in panic, and snorted. The moment it did so, April stopped in her tracks and her face fell.

'Hang on!' she said. 'There's something wrong! Did you see that? This horse has got front teeth!'

She lifted its upper lip, soft and blubbery. There indeed was a respectable set of large, yellowy-green teeth.

'It isn't Angel Pie,' said April, and for a moment Wally had the terrible feeling that April was going to cry. But she didn't.

She frowned, clenched her fists and screwed up her eyes in a determined sort of way. '*Any horse is better than no horse!*' she said.

'What do you mean, April?' asked her aunt.

'Well, the races start in half an hour. I'm never going to find Angel Pie in that time, so I'll ride this horse instead! He's grey, so the stewards won't know any better! Who knows? It might well be my lucky break into horse-racing after all!'

'That's the spirit, April!' said her aunt – she liked people with plenty of spirit. 'I'll bomb off home with Wally – we'll pick up a spare can of petrol – and then we must collect the Bishop. You ride straight to the point-to-point field. We'll see you later!'

With an ear-cracking roar, she and Wally were gone.

Ten minutes later they were standing on the steps of the Bishop's Palace, ringing the doorbell.

The Bishop himself came to the door. He didn't look very happy.

'Oh, Mishes Pwatt . . . there you are. I'm sho nerversh! How can I be sheen wivout my teef! I really don't know if I can go froo wiv it! Hello, Wallash,' he added.

'Oh-dear-oh-lor,' said Vera, who could see that the Bishop had quite a problem.

'Teeth are no problem!' said Wally Pratt suddenly, surprising both his mother and the Lord Bishop.

'Don't be so cheeky, Wally! Whatever do you mean?' said Vera.

'Well, it's easy to make a quick set of false teeth. We do it every day in the playground at school.'

'I shay! Do you really?' A pink smile lit the Bishop's face.

'Yeah. All you need is a penknife and some orange-peel. You turn the peel white side out, cut

out some nice big teeth, and stick them in your gob.
It's easy!'

And so it was, that on the dot of two o'clock, a
magnificent motorbike and side-car, driven by a
housewife in red racing leathers, with her fat son on
the pillion, drew into the VIP car-park at the
point-to-point.

In the side-car sat a bishop with rather a forced
grin on his face, and a white, beaming, goofy smile
across his reverent lips.

14

An Afternoon at the Races

The sky was blue, the day was warm and the afternoon seemed set for a very pleasant point-to-point.

Wally Pratt got off the pillion of his mother's motorbike and went in search of Bean Pole, Bill Stickers and Ginger Tom. He soon found them, and the four boys leaned over the rails at the course's most vicious fence, while Wally told them about the grey horse in the garage and April's determination to run it in the last race.

Mrs Pratt stayed close to the Bishop as he sat in a small grandstand that had been built near the winners' enclosure. Beside it was an area where several bookmakers had put up their betting stalls.

As we already know, Vera doesn't care for horses, or racing, so she spent most of the afternoon simply hoping that the Bishop's orange-peel teeth would last out to the end of the prize-giving ceremony. She doubted if they would.

★   ★   ★

Mr Dud Cheque had a very busy afternoon. Ever since the start of the point-to-point, people had been coming up to Honest Bert's betting stall to put money on Dirty Beast in the last race! By the time everything was ready for the race to begin, Dud was standing guard over two large trunks, full of notes and coins.

'Good afternoon once again, ladies and gentlemen!' said the voice on the public-address system. 'We now come to the last race of the afternoon – the one you've all been waiting for. The runners and riders are just going down to the start now, and very soon they'll be off!'

'Where is she, then?' said Bean Pole, as the horses for the last race trotted past them down towards the start.

'How should I know?' replied Wally. 'She'll be there all right, just you see.'

Sure enough, behind most of the field, there was April.

'There she is!' said Ginger Tom, 'On that big grey horse. Are you sure it's not really hers, Wally?'

'Well, *she* is. Says it's something to do with teeth.'

'It looks very like her horse to me!' added Bean Pole.

The boys could not quite see the start, which was round a curve in the track, but a loudspeaker on a pole just behind them told them what was going on:

'Right, ladies and gentlemen, the horses seem nearly ready for the off. There's Danny Boy, and Proper Charlie, and Teacher's Pet. And I can see the favourite, Dirty Beast, with his jockey in red and yellow. And there's the outsider, the grey, Angel Pie, being ridden by the youngest jockey in today's races, Miss April Phoole. They're under starter's orders . . . THEY'RE OFF!'

A thundering of hoofs on fresh green grass shook the afternoon air.

The loudspeaker went frantic: 'Andatthefirstjump it'sTeacher'sPetfromPrunesandCustardandProper Charlie on the inside. And at the second fence it's still Teacher'sPetandTootiFruiti'safallerthere.'

The boys, at the third fence, craned forward over the railings as the runners and riders poured over the top of it.

'There she is!' yelled Wally, pointing to April as the horses thundered passed. 'She must be about fourth!'

'GO FOR IT, APRIL!' shouted the boys, as the horses' backsides galloped away in a flurry of flying turf.

'Andthey'realloverthethirdjumpfirsttimeround. DirtyBeastinthemiddleofthepack!'

'How many times do they come round?' asked Bean Pole.

'Twice.' said Wally. 'Next time's the last lap.'

Up in the tiny grandstand, Mrs Vera Pratt forgot, temporarily, about the Bishop's frail teeth and surveyed the scene. It was all very pleasant, even though personally she would have much preferred to be watching motorbike racing.

Her eyes moved from a distant part of the field where the horse-boxes were parked, and she gazed in a relaxed way at the winners' enclosure laid out before them. She couldn't help noticing a large van that had pulled up beside one of the betting stalls: it had A B C GARAGE – *for Petrol and Repairs* painted on the side of it. She wondered what it was doing there.

The horses, meanwhile, were now on the start of their last lap. Within moments they were streaming once more over the jump in front of the boys. Teacher's Pet came over first, then Proper Charlie and then two horses together.

'Andtwohorsesareequalthird. It'sAngelPieandthefavouriteDirtyBeast . . . AND DIRTY BEAST IS DOWN! THE FAVOURITE IS OUT OF IT!'

The voice of the loudspeaker was right!

Slimey O'Reilly had done a pretty good job keeping his disguised horse up with the leaders. He had instructions from Captain Smoothy-Smythe to fade back towards the last fences, but the horse seemed to be unstoppable! The moment it had spotted the grey horse with the small girl on it, it had taken off like a rocket!

Slimey, no great jockey, had lost what little control he had. The horse's front legs had crumpled on landing, and before the boys' eyes, horse and rider rolled in a confused heap on the grass!

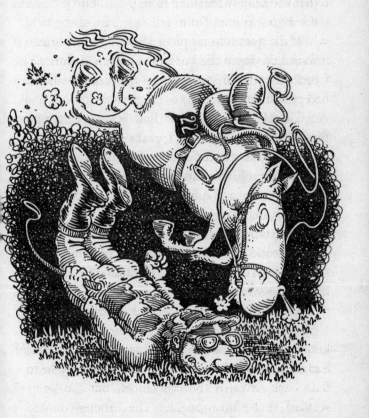

Runners and riders behind streamed over the fence, narrowly missing Slimey, who crouched in a ball and muttered some words to himself that are too rude to print here.

Seconds later, all was silence, save for a murmur in the crowd as hundreds of hopeful people realized that the money they had invested on Dirty Beast in the 4.30 was gone for ever.

The chestnut horse picked itself up and trotted off round the fence and back the way it had come. The jockey, in his distinctive red-and-yellow silks, lay very still on the grass.

'Come on!' said Bean Pole – a very common expression of his. 'Let's see if he's OK.'

The boys ducked under the railing and ran to where the injured man lay. As they got up to him he slowly sat up and rubbed his head.

'Are you all right?' asked Wally.

'Yes, ta,' said Slimey.

He stood up, raised his goggles and limped off in the general direction of the chestnut-brown horse.

Just as Wally was about to follow his friends back to the railing, something pink lying in the grass caught his eye.

He bent down and picked it up. It was a set of rather grassy false teeth.

15

Weird!

'Hey!' shouted Wally Pratt to his three friends. 'This is a bit weird! Here's a pair of false teeth.'

'What's weird about that?' said Bean Pole. 'They probably fell out when the jockey fell off.'

'They didn't,' said Wally. 'Because when he spoke to me just now he wasn't missing any – not this lot anyway – there's a full row of choppers here!'

'Well, so what?' asked Ginger Tom.

'Well . . .' said Wally, 'the Bishop has lost his teeth. I know because I had to show him how to make orange-peel ones. I suppose these could be his.'

'Don't be a wally, Wally!' said Bean Pole. 'How would they get into the middle of a race-track?'

'Search me,' said Wally, 'but I'm going to go and see if they're his.'

'Please yourself!' said Bean Pole. 'Ginger and Bill

and I will see if we can help catch that loose horse. See you later!'

They set off to follow the red-and-yellow jockey and the chestnut horse with the white flash down its forehead.

Wally turned the other way, towards the finish. As he walked he concentrated once more on the public-address system. He could hardly believe what he heard!

'Well, there you are, ladies and gentlemen. A quite remarkable result to the last race today. Angel Pie the winner, a complete outsider, ridden and owned by April Phoole, with Dirty Beast, the favourite, falling four from home.'

April had won! Wally was amazed – so amazed that he almost broke into a trot himself!

He found the Bishop standing with his mother by a table with several cups and shields on it. They were deep in conversation.

'I don't know how I can go froo wiv it!' the Bishop was saying. He was grinning as hard as he could, in order to keep what was left of his orange-peel teeth in. They looked as if they had come to the end of their useful life. Two at the front had fallen off and the rest looked decidedly soggy.

'Look, Mum!' said Wally, interrupting. 'I've just found these false teeth in the middle of the race-track!'

'Let me shee!' said the Bishop. 'Heavens above! They look like mine!' He snatched them, rather abruptly for a bishop, and, discarding the orange-peel, stuffed them into his mouth.

He made a lot of chumbley noises, and grimaced a bit, as if he'd bitten his tongue, but then he spoke: 'Where did you say you found these teeth?'

It was obvious to Vera and her son that these were more or less the Bishop's own teeth. They didn't seem to fit at all well, and they had bits of grass and mud on them, but he did look more like his old self.

'They were in the middle of the track. I spotted them after we all went to help Dirty Beast's jockey when he fell.'

'Bishop,' said Wally's mother in a determined voice. 'Something fishy is going on!'

As she said it the Bishop saw something that very nearly caused him to open his mouth wide with surprise. He only just stopped himself.

Not far from where they were standing, he saw the proprietor of the ABC Garage, Captain Smoothy-Smythe, climbing into the back of his old van.

In his hand he had an old plastic shopping-bag – the one the Bishop had dropped in the betting shop the day before!

16

Postpone the Prizes!

The Captain did not know that he'd been noticed. While everybody else, including Honest Bert himself, had been concentrating on the race, the Captain had spent a happy half hour transferring hundreds of pounds from the trunks at the back of Honest Bert's betting stall to the back of his van. To avoid looking suspicious, he had used an old plastic shopping-bag that Dud Cheque had lent him.

'Good work, Cheque, old man,' hissed the Captain to his partner in crime. 'This is the last load. Then I think we'd better make our getaway. I don't like the idea of all this cash lying around in the back of the jolly old van where any thief could get his dirty little hands on it!' He had a laugh at his own jolly little joke.

On the other side of the winners' enclosure, the Bishop could hardly believe his eyes!

'Mrs Pratt! Look!' he said. 'Look – Captain Smoothy-Smythe has got my wife's plastic shopping-bag – the one I dropped, and he's talking to that ghastly little man who pinched my petrol and captured my teeth in the betting shop!'

He and Vera watched as the Captain and Dud Cheque climbed into the cab of the van, started the engine, and drove it out of the main gate.

'RIGHT!' said Vera Pratt, 'Follow me!'

'But, Mrs Pratt, I'll have to give out the prizes in a moment.'

'Oh, that can wait, we're on to something! Come on!'

She pulled on her crash-helmet and leather gauntlets.

At that moment, Colonel Thundering-Blunderer came up to them. 'Right. Er . . . are you ready for the ceremony, Bishop?'

'It will have to be postponed!' said the Bishop, and he leapt into the side-car.

April, with the mysterious grey horse that had just sped her to victory, was standing at the edge of the enclosure waiting for the ceremony to start.

'Oh, Aunty! I WON! I WON! It's my lucky break into big-time racing!' she squealed delightedly, as her aunt vaulted on to the motorbike.

'Never mind that now, April!' said Vera. 'Get on that horse, quick, and follow that van. We're on to something fishy!'

She kicked the engine into life and revved it furiously. The Bishop pulled on his helmet and, like something in a motorbike scramble, they shot off across the field.

April leapt on to the grey horse.

'Where are you going?' Wally said to her as his extraordinary mother and the Bishop left in a cloud of smoke.

'Quick, Wally,' said April, 'your mum and the Bishop are on to something fishy. We've got to follow that van!' And she galloped off across the field.

Wally looked around for some means of transport.

Leaning against the corner of Honest Bert's betting stall was a rather rusty old bike. Without further thought he ran to it, swung his leg over the saddle and, with the squeak and crunch of an unoiled bicycle, he too set out across the point-to-point field, towards the gate.

Police Sergeant Ivor Truncheon had not had a very busy afternoon. For most of the time he had been standing around in the sunshine, thoroughly enjoying himself. However, he had just finished helping April to get her horse through the crowds of people from the finishing line to the winners' enclosure, and he was now having a chat with a new young policeman, called Andy Cuff, who had just joined the force.

'Hey, Sarge! Did you see that?' said the new recruit, suddenly interrupting him.

'See what?' asked Ivor Truncheon.

'That lad there – he just removed that bike from Honest Bert's betting stall – I reckon he's nicked it!'

'Has he indeed!' said Ivor. 'Right! On our bikes! We will pursue the felon and apprehend him!'

The two officers of the law leapt aboard their large, upright, navy-blue bicycles, and they too set off across the field.

17

Back at the Garage

The van turned out of the race field and headed in the direction of the A B C Garage.

So did the motorbike and side-car, so did April, on the grey horse, and so did Wally on Dud Cheque's bike.

At the back of the procession were the two policemen.

However, down at the A B C Garage, things had been happening.

For a start, Angel Pie, in his chestnut car-paint, had arrived there. This was because after he had fallen and deposited Slimey O'Reilly on the grass, he had decided – as most horses would – that it was now time for tea. He headed back to the garage because he remembered that that was where he had had his bucket of breakfast oats.

He had been followed to the garage, not only by his badly shaken jockey, but also by Bean Pole, Bill Stickers and Ginger Tom, who were trying to catch the horse.

When Angel Pie got to the missing side door of the workshop, he trotted in and tucked into his tea-time bucket.

Slimey trotted in after him. And the boys ran in after Slimey.

'Here,' said Slimey to them, 'we don't want kids round here. You can all push off now!'

'We were only trying to help you catch your racehorse,' replied Bean Pole, a bit annoyed.

'Well, I've got him now, thanks, so push off, all of you!'

'Coo, that's a bit off!' said Ginger Tom to his two friends, as they all walked out of the workshop. 'We were only trying to help!'

'Yeah,' agreed Bill Stickers. 'We followed that horse all the way from the race field. It must be nearly two miles.'

The three of them walked round the front of the garage.

When they were quite near the petrol pumps, on the forecourt, Bean Pole thought he heard a strange sound.

'What was that?' he said.

'What was what?'

'That noise.'

'What noise? I didn't hear anything,' said Bill.

They stopped moving and listened.

Then they all heard it: a low, groaning sound. It seemed to be coming from the garage itself.

The three boys timidly peered through the window at the front of the building. They looked into the office of Captain Smoothy-Smythe.

You may be able to guess what they saw. There, on the floor, with their hands tied behind their backs and gags in their mouths, were two men. One was dressed quite well, in a nice tweed jacket. The other was dressed in jockey underpants.

They were both tied to the legs of the large, untidy desk that stood in the middle of the room.

The men looked up when the boys' shadows fell across the window, and they jerked their heads – indicating that they needed help.

'Come on!' said Bean Pole.

The top portion of the window was open. Bean Pole and Bill Stickers lifted Ginger Tom, because he was the smallest, until he could get his arm through and reach down and open the main window from the inside.

Moments later, the boys were in the office untying the two men. Pete Bogg and Twisty Turner were pleased to see them, but they both felt extremely odd.

Have you ever been coshed with a starting-handle and then had half a bottle of gin poured down your throat?

Neither have I.

'Cor . . .' said Twisty, as the gag came off. 'My nut don't half hurt! And my mouth feels like the bottom of a birdcage!'

'You're not the only one, Turner,' said Pete Bogg. 'I feel as if I've been nutted by a rhino! Where are we, anyway?'

'Shh . . .' said Bean Pole. 'You are at the A B C Garage . . . we don't know what's going on – we came here because we were helping Mr Twisty Turner to catch Dirty Beast. He was favourite in the last race at the point-to-point, but he fell!'

'WHAT!' exclaimed Twisty Turner and Pete

Bogg together. Before Bean Pole could repeat what he had said, they were on their feet.

'Hey!' said Twisty. 'I'd like a word with this so-called Twisty Turner!'

'So would I!' said Pete Bogg.

'Well, he's in the workshop, round the back, with his horse,' said Bill Stickers.

'Come on!' said Pete Bogg, and, finding that the office door into the garage was locked, they all five climbed out of the window.

At the very moment they were all through it, including Twisty Turner in his underpants, and were standing on the garage forecourt, they were joined by the garage van.

It had just driven back from the race field.

18

More Dental Problems for the Bishop

The van swung in beside the petrol pumps and screeched to a halt. The Captain was anxious to get the money from the back of it into the safe in his office as quickly as he could.

He had got down from the passenger seat and opened the back doors before he realized that he was not alone. Three boys and two men were approaching him, and it wasn't very difficult for the Captain to identify the men! Earlier that morning he had personally supervised having them struck over the head with a starting-handle.

It wasn't very difficult for the men to identify the Captain.

'Oi!' shouted Pete Bogg, very loudly. 'We'd like a word with you!' He and the underpanted Twisty Turner advanced across the forecourt.

Dud Cheque was still sitting in the driver's seat of the garage van. In a crisis Dud doesn't have great presence of mind: he's inclined to panic, and that's what he did now.

'It's the owner and jockey!' he screamed. 'GET BACK IN THE VAN, BOSS!'

'I'LL GET YOU!' yelled Twisty Turner, and he ran towards the Captain with his fists clenched. 'I'M GOING TO TURN YOU INSIDE OUT!'

All the noise disturbed Slimey O'Reilly and Angel Pie in the workshop, where they were resting after a busy afternoon. Slimey ran out to see what was going on, and Angel Pie trotted after him.

The real Twisty Turner and Pete Bogg were almost up to the Captain, and were just about to start turning him inside out, when Slimey O'Reilly came round the corner of the garage shouting, 'What the heck's going on here?'

This was a bad mistake because, as you will remember, he was still dressed in Twisty Turner's jockey outfit.

Twisty and Pete swung round.

'Who does he think HE is?' shouted Twisty to Pete Bogg.

'I think he thinks he's YOU!'

'And he's got our horse!'

'Right, let's get him!' shouted Pete Bogg.

And he and Twisty Turner left the Captain in temporary peace, and advanced, shouting rude things, towards the startled Slimey O'Reilly.

I say that the Captain was left in temporary peace because at that very moment a large motorbike and side-car skidded into the garage beside him. It came to a halt by crashing into the side of the van, coming to rest beside the passenger door. It therefore blocked the Captain's way back inside the vehicle.

This was a pity for the Captain, because the brightest idea he had at that moment was to get back into the van and scarper as fast as it would carry him.

'Oi!' shouted Mrs Vera Pratt and the Lord Bishop

together. 'We'd like a word with you!' They pointed at Captain Smoothy-Smythe.

This exclamation surprised Pete Bogg and Twisty Turner, causing them to look round before beginning the task of taking Slimey O'Reilly to pieces. The split-second pause gave Slimey the chance to do something intelligent.

He leapt on to the back of the weary Angel Pie, dug his heels into the poor animal's flanks, and set off like a rocket towards the hedge at the far side of the ABC Garage. He and the horse disappeared across it like something from the Grand National.

Twisty and Pete saw that Slimey had got away, and they turned round again with a view to resuming the job of dismantling Captain Smoothy-Smythe.

Unlikely though it sounds, Dud Cheque then did something fairly sensible. Mrs Pratt was sitting on her motorbike, pointing at the Captain in an aggressive way, and she was only a foot or two from where Dud was sitting in the driving seat.

He moved across the cab and, with all his might, he flung open the van door. It caught Vera on the back of the head, and she slumped forward, senseless, over the handlebars of her beloved bike.

The Bishop was just climbing out of the side-car when this happened, and the door missed him by inches. He was horrified.

'Now, look here!' he said sternly to the Captain. 'I strongly suspect that you and this ghastly little man,' he pointed at Dud Cheque, 'are in criminal collusion! I believe he pinched my teeth and my wife's plastic shopping-bag! I'd like to look in the back of this van! You are up to something fishy!'

The Bishop was now standing between the Captain and the open door of the van, and Twisty Turner and Pete Bogg could be heard approaching from behind.

The Captain did a very wicked thing: 'Get out of my way, you jolly old blighter!' he snarled, and he socked the Bishop on the jaw.

There was a sound like crunching gravel. Bits of false teeth flew in every direction, and the Bishop sat down on the forecourt in stunned amazement.

Then April Phoole arrived, at the gallop, on Dirty Beast.

19

They're Off!

'Hey!' said April. 'What's going on here?'

She surveyed the scene. The three boys were standing, amazed, by the petrol pumps. Two men – one dressed only in underpants – were shouting and rushing around clenching their fists, her aunt's motorbike and side-car were jammed up against the garage van and she was slumped, lifeless, over the handlebars, and a toothless bishop was sitting on the forecourt. It would have been enough to make anyone ask what was going on.

April jumped down from the back of Dirty Beast and ran to her slumbering aunt.

The Captain, having removed the obstacle of the Bishop, leapt up into the van.

'Right, Cheque! Let's get out of here, jolly pronto!'

There was a smell of burning rubber as Dud Cheque revved the engine, and smoke poured out from under the bonnet, but the getaway van would not get away! Vera's mighty motorbike had struck it so hard that the van's front wing was crushed against the front wheel, locking it solid.

'I'll get you now!' shouted Pete Bogg, and he jumped over the motorbike and tore at the handle of the van's passenger door.

Twisty picked up a white painted stone from the forecourt grass and smashed the windscreen with it. 'I'll teach you to pinch my jockey outfit!' he shouted. 'We're going to take you two to pieces!'

While Pete and Twisty were getting on with getting at the unfortunate Captain and rotten little Dud Cheque, a face suddenly looked up over the hedge at the far side of the garage. It belonged to a horse, and when it threw back its head and whinnied at April Phoole, she instantly saw that it had no front teeth.

'THERE'S ANGEL PIE!' she squealed with delight.

She was right. Slimey O'Reilly may have disappeared over the hedge on Angel Pie like something in the Grand National, but what no one had seen was that they had both landed head-first in a small, dank pond on the other side of it.

For the second time that afternoon, Slimey had fallen from the back of Angel Pie, but this time he had not landed on grass.

The pond was black and foul and stinking, and at that very moment, Slimey was sitting in it.

'There's Angel Pie!' April repeated, and the horse, recognizing its long-lost owner, barged its way back through the hedge and trotted towards her.

The pond water seemed to have had some effect on his paintwork; large patches of grey were showing through the chestnut.

'He's been painted!' shouted April.

Things were happening in the front of the van. Pete Bogg had got the passenger door open, and Twisty Turner had made a hole in the windscreen large enough for a small jockey to dive through.

The Captain realized that in this situation the best form of defence is to make a run for it.

'Open your door, Cheque, you imbecile, and let's get out of here!'

Dud did as he was told.

The wicked pair slipped out of the driver's door, ran round the back of the van, and before Pete Bogg, or Twisty Turner, or April, or the boys, or the toothless Bishop, or the senseless Vera Pratt, or even Angel Pie could do anything about it, they had jumped up on to the back of the real Dirty Beast.

The Captain was in front, in the saddle, and Dud clung on behind him.

'Right! Jolly well tally ho!' yelled Captain Smoothy-Smythe.

He dug his suede shoes into the favourite's sides, and Dirty Beast stepped out into the road.

20

They're Off Again!

At almost the same time as Captain Smoothy-Smythe and Dud Cheque, on the real Dirty Beast, stepped out into the road and prepared to make their getaway, Wally Pratt, on Dud Cheque's bike, came over the brow of the hill above the garage.

Not very far behind him were the two officers of the law, Police Sergeant Ivor Truncheon and Police Constable Andy Cuff.

Wally came down the hill as fast as the ancient bike would carry him. As you know, he is a heavy child, and as he approached the garage he was doing a very respectable thirty-five miles an hour.

As you also know, the bike has no brakes.

One of the good things about Wally Pratt is that when he puts his mind to it, he really throws his weight into things.

A moment later he threw his weight into Captain Smoothy-Smythe and Dud Cheque.

There was no way Wally could stop. One minute the road was empty, the next there was a large grey horse with a white mane running across it, with two determined criminals on it.

When he hit them, Wally and the bicycle parted company: the bike went straight under the horse, between its front and back legs, and came to a jangling halt in the middle of the road a bit further on.

Wally, however, went *over* the horse. He took off like a heavyweight rocket, and on his journey across the horse's back he knocked its two riders clean off, and on to the ground. They broke his fall, and, before he quite knew where he was, he was sitting in the road beside the horse, on top of them.

As the dust settled, the two policemen arrived on the scene.

'Now then!' said Ivor, 'It looks to me as if someone has been riding a bike without due care and attention!' He began to take out a notebook.

'Wait a minute!' interrupted April. 'Look at the horse!' and she pointed at the bewildered Dirty Beast.

He was in quite a sweat, what with winning a race, being used to chase villains, and being run into by Wally Pratt, but the remarkable thing was that behind the saddle, where Dud had been sitting, he was no longer grey!

The effect of Dud's trouser-legs on the horse's sweaty sides had removed the paint! Two chestnut leg marks were clearly visible.

'He's been painted!' shouted April in a shrill voice, for the second time that afternoon. '*That's why there were all those empty grey paint tins round the side of the garage! These men are crooks!*'

'You bet they are!' said Twisty Turner. 'They pinched my outfit – and our horse!'

'They hit us on the nut and tied us up!' added Pete Bogg.

The Bishop, sitting in the road, had not said anything for a while. If you are a bishop, you are not used to being given a right uppercut to the jaw – and he was still getting over the surprise of it. However, he heard all that was being said, and he decided that the time had come to use his full authority.

'Offishers,' he said, 'arresht vose two villains!'

'Very well, Your Holiness' said Sergeant Truncheon.

A second later, Captain Smoothy-Smythe and Dud Cheque were sitting in the road, handcuffed, back-to-back.

Ivor Truncheon took out his notebook. 'Mr Captain Smoothy-Smythe,' he said in an official tone, 'Irishstew in the name of the law, for painting horses what don't belong to you!'

'Ver's more van vat!' said the Bishop excitedly, not seeming to care any longer about his lack of teeth. 'Vey pinched my petwol, and my teef, and my plastic shopping-bag! Vey used it to put somfing in ver back of viss van! It'sh all very sushpishush!'

Andy Cuff, who was a very keen young policeman, ran to the back of the van.

'He's right, Sarge!' said Andy. 'The back of this van is full of cash!' He was exaggerating, but there were hundreds and hundreds of pounds in bags and bundles of notes on the floor of the van.

'Anover fing,' said the Bishop, just remembering it, 'VEY'VE JUST SMASHED MY FALSH TEEF! AND WHAT ABOUT POOR MISHES PWATT?'

'Who?' asked Sergeant Truncheon.

'Mishes Pwatt,' repeated the Bishop.

'Who is Mishes Pwatt?'

'That lady there is!' said Wally, who had now dusted himself down a bit and had sorted out where he was. He pointed to Vera's unconscious red-leather form, still slumped over the handlebars of the motorbike. 'She's my mum!'

The policemen, the Bishop, April, Pete Bogg, Twisty Turner, Wally and the three boys all gathered round the wrecked bike and side-car. Ivor Truncheon lifted Vera's head slightly and looked into her eyes. They were open, and gently rolling.

She groaned, then she spoke: 'Right!' she said. 'Let's get back to the point-to-point! I've got some business to finish!' and she sat up.

The reason for her remarkable recovery is easy to explain. When the van door had caught her on the back of her head, she still had her crash-helmet on. The blow had dazed her, but no real damage had been done. The Captain could have told Dud Cheque that for the van door to have had full effect, the crash-helmet needed to be removed first.

Ivor Truncheon spoke: 'These two felons will accompany us to the station to help us with our enquiries into why they shouldn't have a very hefty fine to pay!'

'And,' said the Bishop, 'I musht get back to ver races to give out ver pwyshes!'

21

Prizes and Rewards!

So it was, that as the sun began to cast long shadows across the winners' enclosure, a large horse-box drew once more into the point-to-point field.

It had *Dirty Beast – Everyone's Favourite* painted on the side of it and it was being driven by Twisty Turner, in his underpants.

In the cab beside him sat the Lord Bishop, Wally Pratt and his red-leather mum.

In the back, sitting on the strawy floor, were Captain Smoothy-Smythe and Dud Cheque in handcuffs: they were closely guarded by Sergeant Truncheon and PC Andy Cuff. Beside them sat Pete Bogg, April Phoole, Bean Pole, Bill Stickers and Ginger Tom.

The horse-box drew up beside the winners' enclosure, and everyone got out. The Captain and Dud Cheque were swiftly transferred into the back of a large black police van, and the last I heard of them, they were answering some very tricky questions down at the local police station.

'Ah . . . There you are, Bishop!' said Colonel Thundering-Blunderer. 'We've been waiting for you! We're all ready for the prize ceremony now!'

'Sho am I,' replied the Bishop.

'I won't be a moment, Bishop,' whispered Mrs Pratt. 'I'll meet you back here when you've finished!'

The Bishop followed the Colonel to the front of the small grandstand. Some speeches were made about what an excellent day's racing there had been, and everyone clapped politely.

Then the Bishop was announced, and, as Colonel Thundering-Blunderer called out the names, the Bishop gave out cups and trophies to the winners of every race.

'And now,' said the Colonel into a microphone, 'we come to the last race of the day!' A ripple of excitement went round the crowd. 'The winner was a complete outsider, Angel Pie, ridden by the youngest jockey in the races today – Miss April Phoole!'

People clapped enthusiastically – even those who had lost large sums of money on Dirty Beast. April stepped forward and received a huge cup from the Bishop, who spoke softly to her: 'Shimply

shooper . . .' he said. 'Congwatulashons!'

When the ceremony was over, the Bishop met up with Mrs Pratt, as arranged. He was not looking very happy.

'What's up, Bish!' she asked.

'Well, it'sh all very well!' said the Bishop. 'I'm glad vose cwiminals have been caught, but what *ish* my wife going to shay when she sees me? I've losht my teef for good, and she's bound to mish her shopping-bag!' He rubbed his badly bruised chin thoughtfully.

'Don't you fret about that, Bishop,' said Vera cheerfully. 'I've got a nice little surprise for you. My Wally and me have just been over to Honest Bert's betting stall, and collected our winnings!'

'Winningsh?'

'Yes, winnings! You see, I put a bet on April in the last race – after all, she is my niece – it was the least I could do for her: *somebody* had to bet on the poor girl.'

The Bishop's mouth opened in amazement.

'I didn't have any spare money, so I was a bit naughty and used your ten pounds' petrol money! I gave it to Honest Bert himself, yesterday, through the side door of his betting shop while you were in the front. That's why I wasn't around when you came out. I got odds of a hundred to one!'

'Pleeshe wemind me: what dush vat mean?'

'It means, Bish, that for every pound I put on, I won a hundred back! I've just picked up a thousand pounds from Honest Bert!'

The Bishop's mouth opened even wider.

'The point is, though,' said Vera quietly, 'I realize now that the money wasn't really mine in the first place: it was yours, and I should have bought petrol with it!'

She put her hand into a pocket, deep inside her red-leather jacket, and brought out a fat bundle of fifty-pound notes.

'Here you are, Bishop,' she said.

'Oh, Mishes Pwatt, I can't take it! You won it! It'sh yoursh!'

He pushed the money back towards her.

'Tell you what,' said Vera. 'We're both a bit short of cash. How say we split it and have half each?'

'Shimply shplendid!' replied the Bishop, and he smiled at her and Wally Pratt with a broad pink smile.